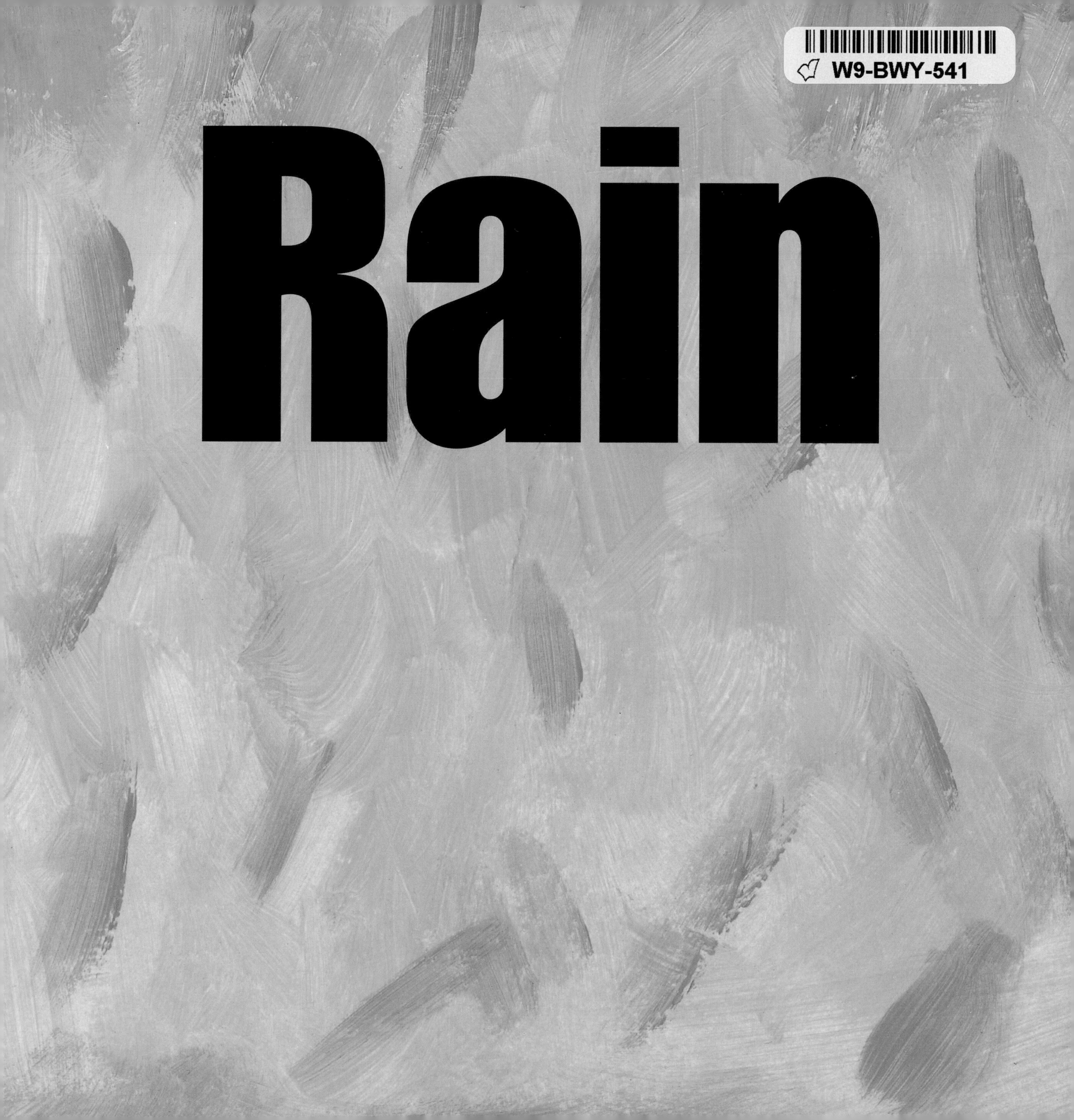
Rain

In memory of my dad, Lyuba, with whom
I enjoyed watching thunderstorms.

Published by Dragonfly Books
an imprint of Random House Children's Books
a division of Random House, Inc., New York

Originally published in hardcover in the United Kingdom by David Bennett Books Limited in 2000.
Published in hardcover by Crown Publishers, an imprint of Random House Children's Books, in 2000.
This edition published by arrangement with Crown Publishers.

Visit us on the Web! www.randomhouse.com/kids
Educators and librarians, for a variety of teaching tools, visit us at www.randomhouse.com/teachers

The Library of Congress has cataloged the hardcover edition of this work as follows:
Stojic, Manya.
Rain / written and illustrated by Manya Stojic.
p. cm.
Summary: The animals of the African savanna use their senses to predict and then enjoy the rain.
ISBN: 978-0-517-80085-0 (trade)—ISBN: 978-0-517-80086-7 (lib. bdg.)
[1. Rain and rainfall—Fiction. 2. Zoology—Africa—Fiction.
3. Senses and sensation—Fiction. 4. Africa—Fiction.] I. Title.
PZ7.S873Rai 2000
[E]—dc21 99035298

ISBN: 978-0-385-73729-6 (pbk.)
Reprinted by arrangement with Crown Books for Young Readers
MANUFACTURED IN CHINA
First Dragonfly Books Edition
April 2009
10 9 8 7 6 5 4 3 2 1

Random House Children's Books supports the First Amendment and celebrates the right to read.

WRITTEN AND ILLUSTRATED BY

MANYA STOJIC

It was hot.

Everything was hot and dry.

The red soil was hot and dry and cracked.

A porcupine sniffed around.

"It's time,"

she whispered.

"The rain

is coming!

I can smell it.

I must tell the zebras."

Lightning **flashed.**

"The rain is coming!"

said the zebras.

"Porcupine can smell it.
We can **see** it. We must
tell the **baboons.**"

Thunder
boomed.

"The rain is coming!"
cried the baboons.

"Porcupine
can smell it.
The zebras
can see it.
We can **hear** it.
We must tell
the **rhino.**"

A raindrop **splashed.**

"The rain is here!"

said the rhino.

"Porcupine smelled it.

The zebras saw it.

The baboons heard it.

And I **felt** it.
I must tell
the **lion.**”

The lion
spoke
in a
deep
purr.

“Yes, the rain is here.

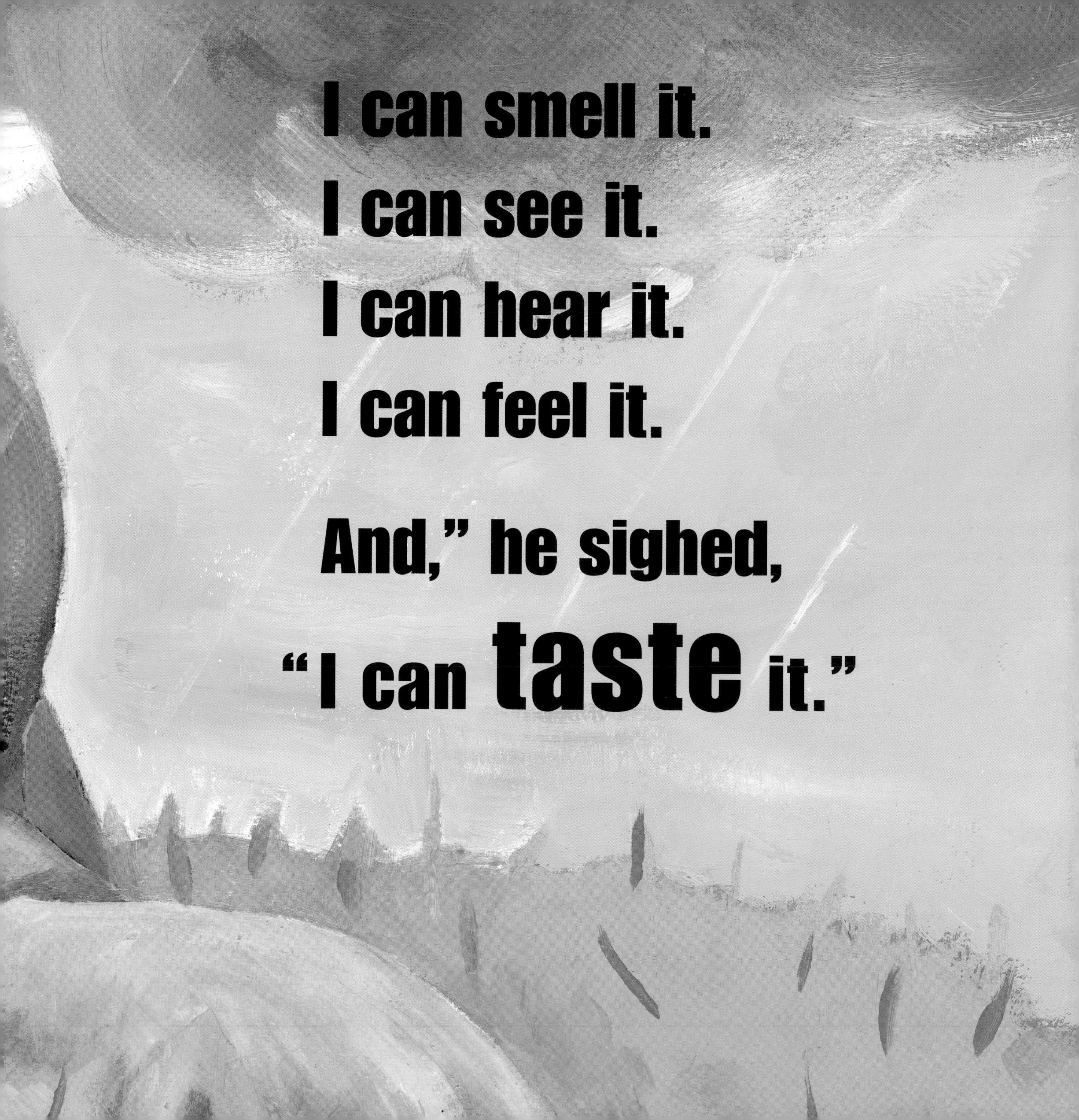

I can smell it.
I can see it.
I can hear it.
I can feel it.

And," he sighed,
"I can **taste** it."

It rained

and it

rained

and it

rained.

It rained until every river

gushed and gurgled.

It rained until every water hole

was full.

Then the rain stopped
and everywhere long,
feathery grasses grew
from the soil.

Every tree began to sprout fresh, green leaves.

"I can't taste
the rain now,"
purred the lion,

"but I can enjoy
the shade of these
big, green
leaves."

"I can't feel the rain now," said the rhino,

"but I can lie in the

cool, soft, squelchy mud."

"We can't hear the rain now,"
shouted the baboons,

"but we can eat

fresh,

juicy fruit

from the trees."

"We can't see
the rain now,"
said the zebras,

"but we can have
a **refreshing**
drink from
the water hole."

"I can't smell the rain now,"
whispered the porcupine,
"but **I know** that it will
come back again.
When it's
time."

The sun shone over the plain.

It was **hot.**

Everything was drying out.

The red soil was hot and dry.

A tiny crack appeared.